WITHDRAWN

By Jasmine Jones

miramax books

HYPERION
New York

If you purchased this book without a cover, you should be aware that this book is stolen property. It was reported as "unsold and destroyed" to the publisher, and neither the author nor the publisher has received any payment for this "stripped" book.

The "ARCHIE" property and associated character names and likenesses TM and © Archie Comic Publications, Inc., 2004, and are used under license by Diamond Select Toys and Collectibles, LLC.
All rights reserved.

The original ARCHIE characters were conceived by John Goldwater and drawn by Bob Montana for Archie Comics.

Visit BETTY & VERONICA® online at
www.archiecomics.com

Volo® is a registered trademark of Disney Enterprises, Inc.
No part of this book may be reproduced or transmitted in any form or by any means, electronic or mechanical, including photocopying, recording, or by any information storage and retrieval system, without written permission from the publisher.
For information address Hyperion Books for Children,
114 Fifth Avenue, New York, New York 10011-5690.

Printed in the United States of America
First Edition, 2005
1 3 5 7 9 10 8 6 4 2

This book is set in 13-point Cheltenham.
ISBN 0-7868-5568-1

Visit www.hyperionbooksforchildren.com

Dear Reader,

Betty and I have been best friends for ages . . . but we still have tons to talk about. In fact, sometimes Daddykins complains because we're on the phone too much.

We wrote this book so that you can see how we have remained friends through the years. I hope these tips inspire you in your friendships! After all, there's no friend like an old friend. . . . (Not that we're old, of course!)

xoxo,
Veronica

Hi, Reader!

You know, Ronnie and I have been friends for years. And it's true—sometimes we fight. But we always make up again.

That's why she and I put together this book—to help other people be the absolute best friends they can be. Ronnie and I are a good example. We're there for each other when things are really rough. And we're there for the fun times, too!

After all, that's what friends are for, isn't it?

Luv ya,
Betty

Friendship

Let Your Friends Know You Care!

Don't wait around for the end of the year to write in your friend's yearbook. Slip your friend a note and let her know why you think she's special!

Hey, Ronnie!
Love your outfit today—it's fab! Want to go shopping together after school? I want to find out where you got your purse so I can write the store up in my fashion 'zine!
xoxo,
Ginger

Hey, Jughead!
Let's go hang out at Pop's after school.
Your pal,
Archie

Betty,
I'm helping the Outdoor Club with their bake sale. Since you're the best cook I know, I was wondering if you wanted to bake up something together. I always know that I can count on you!
Love,
Nancy

Midge,
I just wanted to write you a note and say thanks for listening last night when I called to tell you about the fight I had with my sister. You're such a good friend!
Kisses and hugs,
Betty

Hey, Arch!
Let's round up the gang and head to the beach this weekend. I feel like playing a little volleyball . . . and I need someone to make me look good! (Just kidding, buddy. You know the beach just isn't the same without your best friends!)
Reggie

Betty!
I just bought this fabulous new facial mask—it's suppose to make your skin silky-smoot Why don't you come over late and we'll try it out? (You're th only person I'd let see me wit a face covered with blue goop
Smoochies,
Ronnie

What Makes a Good Friend?

Sometimes people ask me how I can be best friends with Veronica. And I have to admit that she can be a little bit unreasonable sometimes. Like, when we go to the beach, Ronnie expects me to stand around fanning her so that she won't get hot and sweaty and mess up her designer swimsuit. But on the other hand, I was once feeling really down—and Ronnie did everything she could to cheer me up. She even sent over a clown to make me laugh!

So, what makes Ronnie such a great friend?

- She's always honest with me—but not in a hurtful way.
- She knows how to give a compliment.
- She knows how to keep a secret.
- She manages to make every day seem like an adventure.
- She'd do anything to make me smile!

Betty and I are very different. She likes to fix cars. I don't know the difference between a carburetor and a cauliflower. She likes to bake. I don't even know how to boil water. Betty likes to shop—but she doesn't think of fashion as a way of life, like I do.

So, what makes Betty such a great friend?

- She's always ready to tell me how gorgeous I am . . . even when I just got the world's ugliest haircut.

- She's willing to listen . . . for hours.

- She's equally ready to cheer me up or cheer me on.

- She puts up with me . . . even when I'm being a teensy-weensy bit demanding.

- She knows all my faults, and she loves me anyway.

Types of Friends

Not all friends are created equal. For example: Ginger is a great friend of mine; she's fun to hang out with at the beach, or go shopping with, or dance with at a party. But if I have a secret, or something is really bothering me, I'd rather talk to Betty—because she's my best friend. You can have lots of different kinds of friends. And I think we all know that when it comes to variety, I believe in having at least one of everything. Take a look at the list below and see if you recognize any of these types from your circle of friends.

The Fun Friend

Ginger is the kind of friend you can always count on when you want to have a great time—and she's always up for something new. She and I have a lot in common. Her passion is fashion, and so is mine. She also loves to surf, and spend as much time at the beach as possible. She's the perfect person to call when you want to make plans for the weekend. You never know what you'll end up doing, but you know you'll have fun!

The Sweet Friend

It's important to have one friend whom you know you can count on to be understanding whenever you have a problem—who offers a shoulder to cry on. Midge is a total sweetie. She would do anything for a good friend. Whenever Betty or I have a project that we desperately need help with, we know that Midge is the one to call. Her heart is always in the right place.

The Inspirational Friend

When you're feeling down, you need the kind of friend who can snap you out of your funk: someone who will give you a pep talk, put a smile on your face, and make you believe that anything is possible. Brigitte is just that kind of friend. She's made a name for herself in the music business, and she believes in following her dreams, no matter what. Whenever I go off course (not that I so very often, but it does happen!), I know that I can count on Brigitte to get me back on track.

The Forever Friend

There are some people who have been in your life so long you can't even remember how you met them. Nancy is one of those people. Even though she isn't my best friend, she has known me so long that at this point she really understands me. New friends are great, but old ones remind you of how you used to be . . . and how much you've grown.

The Best Friend

What can I say? Betty and I are very different. She loves science; I love shoes. She likes to play sports; I like to watch boys play sports. But no matter how different we are, I know that I can count on Betty to be there for me, no matter what. She's the world's best listener, the world's most generous person, and the world's best friend.

The More the Merrier

Best friends don't always come in a single package. Sometimes, you can have two or more best friends with whom you share all of your crushes, dreams, and secrets. Some people say three is a crowd, but I think that's silly. The truth is, there are certain things you can never have too much of. Like diamonds, cool clothes . . . and, of course, friends!

Best Things About Having More than One Best Friend

❁ Even if one of your best friends is sick, you can still eat lunch with the other one.

❁ There are more buds around to cheer you up when you're feeling down.

❁ If you aren't sure about your new haircut, you can always get a second opinion . . . or a third!

❁ When you all have different interests and ideas, you never fall into a rut.

❁ If you're angry with one best friend, you still have another one to talk to.

❁ Working on a project or throwing a party is way easier with more people!

12

What's Good (and Bad!) About Being Part of a Group of Friends!

You Can:

Go to the game and cheer for your friend as he scores the winning touchdown. A group of friends can make a lot of noise!

But Watch Out:

That your other friends on the football team don't get jealous! Once, when Reggie was injured, Archie took his place as quarterback— and won the big game. The whole Riverdale gang cheered like crazy for Archie . . . but then Reggie felt left out. We should have let Reggie know that we were thinking of him, too!

You Can:

Head to the beach for a full day of fun! In our crowd, Betty brings the beach blanket, Moose brings the football, Jughead keeps an eye out for snacks, Archie makes sure to have a Frisbee, and I make the beach beautiful just by being there!

But Watch Out:

The last time our gang went to the beach, we spent so much time playing Frisbee and football and eating snacks that we completely forgot to go into the water!

You Can:

Plan a superfun makeover party for all of your girlfriends! Once, Betty helped me plan a fantastic makeover-sleepover party. Everyone was there—including Nancy, Midge, and Ethel—and we had a blast trying out everybody's makeup and suggesting new looks to one another.

But Watch Out:

For gate-crashers! When Jughead, Archie, and Reggie heard about the party, they decided that they wanted to come, too. They showed up while we were still in our curlers and mud masks! It was so embarrassing . . . and then Jughead ate all of the snacks! Next time, Betty and I will be sure to throw a party for the whole gang. Trying to leave out the boys just wasn't a good idea!

You Can:

Spend hours hanging out—and never get bored! Our gang always meets up at Pop's for burgers and malts. We can spend all day there, just talking, eating, and playing songs on the jukebox.

But Watch Out:

Don't let Jughead stick you with the bill!

Planning Parties

Ronnie and I just love throwing parties—slumber parties, beach parties, holiday parties . . . you name it! A theme can be a great way to get people excited about hanging out together. Here are a few fun party ideas for you to share with friends!

In the Pink

Invitations: Your invitations can be store-bought or homemade—as long as they're pink! (Or white with pink lettering.)

Food and decorations: Haul out the pink Kool-Aid, strawberry Jell-O, strawberry ice cream, strawberry milk, and cake with strawberry frosting. Decorate with pink streamers and balloons, and plastic pink flamingos, if you have them!

Music: Anything by Pink, of course!

Games and activities: Ask your guests to dress for the theme—in their best pink clothes.

As an activity, you can rent the classic '80s movie *Pretty in Pink*. (Have everyone shout whenever someone in the movie says the word "pink.") Or rent one of the *Pink Panther* movies.

Have your guests bring magazines to use in group crafts. Cut out any pictures with pink objects in them. Use a large piece of poster board or butcher paper to assemble a giant pink collage!

Go Hollywood!

Invitations: Cut out a bunch of "Oscars" from yellow construction paper. Send the awards through the mail, or hand them out in school.

Food and decorations: Place bowls of popcorn around the room (what are movies without popcorn?), and set out trays of finger foods, like crackers and cheese. Cut out movie advertisements from magazines, and tape them to the walls, or decorate walls with movie posters. Play the sound tracks of your favorite movies as your guests arrive.

Games and activities: Have everyone make a name tag with his or her Hollywood name. (Use your middle name as your first name, and the name of the first street you ever lived on as your last name.) Or ask your guests to come dressed as their favorite celebrities!

Play "amnesia." Have one person step out of the room, while the others decide who she is supposed to be (pick a celebrity whom everyone has heard of). Once you've decided, call your friend back into the room, and see if she can guess who she is, using fewer than twenty yes-or-no questions.

You can also schedule your party for the night of an awards show, like the Nickelodeon Kids' Choice Awards. You can watch the show throughout your party!

Luau

Invitations: Send the information on tropical-theme postcards. Be sure to write *"Hele mei hoohiwahi,"* which means "Come Celebrate" in Hawaiian, at the top.

Food and decorations: Ask your parents for help in preparing a giant tropical fruit salad. Use pineapple, papaya, mango, and lots of other tropical fruits. Set out a platter of fresh veggies and dip. Also consider ordering a Hawaiian pizza—made with pineapple and ham, it's surprisingly tasty. For decorations, head to your party store for leis and bright plastic cups with colorful flower motifs.

Music: Pick any sort of tropical or Hawaiian music, or songs by the Beach Boys.

Games and activities: Ask your guests to come dressed in Hawaiian shirts or beach clothes.

Do the limbo! Use a broom or long pole and have your guests line up and shimmy underneath it one by one. After everyone has gone through, lower the pole. The person who can get under the pole at the lowest height (without falling!) is the winner!

Hold a hula-hoop contest.

The Christmas Whenever Party!

Invitations: It may be July, but you're having a Christmas party, so cut green construction paper into the shape of a Christmas tree. Write out the information on the back, then glue colorful beads or glitter on the front (to look like tree decorations).

Food and decorations: The idea is to go holiday-crazy, even if it's the middle of summer! Haul out the holly, put up a wreath, and string up strands of Christmas lights. Serve gingerbread cookies and candy canes.

Music: Christmas carols, of course!

Games and activities: Have all of your guests bring candy, and let everyone build small "gingerbread" houses. Buy tubes of white frosting and a few boxes of graham crackers. Guests can glue the graham-cracker squares together to make mini houses, then decorate the houses with candy.

Ask everyone to bring a small gift (wrapped in holiday paper). Then hold a Secret Santa gift swap!

Rent a stack of your favorite holiday movies, like *A Christmas Story, Home Alone*, or *It's a Wonderful Life.*

Far Out! Space Party

Invitations: Send them by e-mail (of course)! Check out a Web site that has templates for e-cards. Choose one with a cool space theme.

Food and decorations: Bake sugar cookies in the shapes of stars, moons, and planets, and serve with bright blue or yellow soda. Put out a tray of Moon Pies and Milky Way bars. Also serve individual pizzas . . . they're perfect "flying saucers." Decorate the room with silver balloons and glow-in-the-dark star stickers.

Games and activities: Install a black light in your living room, and give guests glow-in-the-dark necklaces as they walk in the door.

Turn off the lights. Have your guests stand in a circle, then hand out three glow-in-the-dark balls. Play a crazy game of hot potato with all three balls in action!

Rent one (or all!) of the *Star Wars* movies.

Hostess Dos and Don'ts

Throwing a party can be a lot of work. But it's a ton of fun if you know what you're doing. Here are a few tips that will ensure that everyone (including you!) will have a good time.

[✔] **Do** send out your invitations early! Give guests at least two weeks to respond.

[✔] **Do** call each of your guests a week before the party to remind them that they are invited and to make sure that they can come. Hey—sometimes invitations get lost in the mail. A phone call is a great way to make sure that nobody's feelings are hurt if her invite didn't show up.

[✔] **Do** say hello to your guests as they arrive.

[✔] **Do** make sure that there are enough party favors for everyone!

[✔] Don't get upset if something goes wrong. People at the party want to see you—nobody cares if the punch doesn't taste perfect. Just laugh off any mistakes, and your guests will laugh with you.

[✔] Don't forget to thank your guests for coming!

Friends Help Out

Top Five Things to Do
When Your Friend Is Blue

Let's face it—life isn't always cookies and ice cream. Sometimes things just don't go according to plan. If you see that your friend is feeling down, you can help. That's when true friendship kicks into high gear. When your friend is sad, or sick, or feeling lonely, you can often make her feel better just by reminding her that you're there for her—no matter what. Here are a few other ideas for what you can do when your friend isn't feeling her best.

Your best friend blew the big math test? Got dissed by a crush? Didn't make the team? Here are a few ideas you can try when your friend is having a beyond-lousy day. . . .

5. Rent a stack of funny movies and join her at her house for a popcorn-and-movie fest. Vow not to leave until she's laughing!

4. Distract your friend with a new activity. Get her out of the house. Try something physical, like in-line skating or snowboarding. She won't be able to think about how miserable she is if she's trying not to fall down.

Besides, studies show that exercise is a great mood-lifter!

3. Picture the future. Get out a stack of magazines and a piece of poster board, then make a collage using images of your best friend with her hot new boyfriend, in next year's cheerleading outfit, hanging at the beach, or receiving the Nobel Prize for physics.

2. Make up a goofy song or rhyme, then leave it on her answering machine. She can play it whenever the blues strike.

And the number-one way to cheer up a friend . . .

1. Listen. Sometimes, all it takes is offering a shoulder to cry on to make your friend feel a whole lot better.

But Definitely Don't . . .

. . . Make your friend feel bluer by telling her all she's missing. This is the time to play Positive Girl and look for the silver lining. Make sure the focus is on your friend . . . she'll appreciate it.

Top Five Things to Do When Your Friend Is Sick

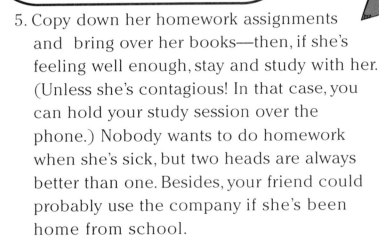

Whether your friend's got a little cold or a broken leg, it's a pain to be down for the count! Your friend is probably missing her buddies and feeling uncomfortable. Here are a few little things you can do to brighten your friend's day while she's recovering from her illness.

5. Copy down her homework assignments and bring over her books—then, if she's feeling well enough, stay and study with her. (Unless she's contagious! In that case, you can hold your study session over the phone.) Nobody wants to do homework when she's sick, but two heads are always better than one. Besides, your friend could probably use the company if she's been home from school.

4. Make a huge "Get Well Soon" card and have all of your friends sign it. Then hand-deliver it to her house. Or send her a funny e-card or e-mail.

3. Give her a makeover gift bag. Being sick can make a person feel seriously yucky. Your

friend would probably love to get a few cool hair clips or some nail polish . . . quick, easy ways to start feeling better about herself.

2. Bring over an easy art project. Something your friend can work on in bed is ideal. You might try a sketch pad, or paint pens to decorate jars or boxes. It's a fun way to take your friend's mind off her illness.

And the number-one thing to do when your friend is sick . . .

1. Give her a book. Having a good book to read will help her pass the time while she is stuck in bed. Why not look on your bookshelf for one of your favorites to share with her? Afterward you can talk about your favorite parts of the story.

But Definitely Don't . . .

. . . Forget about her if it's a long illness. Make sure you call or stop by every day or so. It doesn't have to be a long visit—you just want to let her know that you're thinking of her . . . and hopefully get her to laugh or smile. As they say—laughter is the best medicine!

Top Five Things to Do When Your Friend Is Away

Ah, summer. The sun. The pool. And . . . camp? Oh, no! You and your best bud are going to be spending weeks apart, and you're seriously bumming. What can you do to make sure that she knows you're thinking about her?

5. Before she leaves (or you do), give her a stack of preaddressed and stamped postcards. Then make a stack for yourself, with *her* address.

4. Write her a letter listing all of the things you'll miss about her *before* you part. Then hand it over, but tell her not to open it until she really misses you badly.

3. If you're the one staying home, and she's going to camp, put together a care package. Most camps have rules against candy and cookies, but you can pick up some fun puzzles and toys for her to share with her pals at camp.

2. Make your friend a "hello" note on a plain white T-shirt, using a fabric marker. Get your other buds to sign it, too. Send both the shirt and the pen to your friend and tell her to have her new friends sign it, too! It's a great summer keepsake.

And the top way to keep close with a faraway friend . . .

1. Whether you're at camp or at home, use free time or time in arts and crafts or jewelry-making class to make something for your bud, like a friendship bracelet, a drawing of your camp, or a picture frame. You'll have something for her when you see her again, and she'll know you were missing her!

But Definitely Don't . . .

. . . Spend so much time missing your old friend that you miss out on making new ones! Summer is a great time to have fun with new people. So get out there, be friendly, and don't forget to smile!

Making New Friends

How to Make New Friends

✳ **Join a club.** Your school probably has lots of different clubs—one of them is sure to grab your attention. Make sure that you stick to your interests, though. When Archie and Betty joined the Hiking Club, Ronnie decided to check out the club scene, too. She tried the Cooking Club (ugh!) and the Science Club (yikes!) before finding the Fashion Club (perfect fit!).

✳ **Play a sport.** Betty loves to play basketball, Ronnie is a cheerleader, and Archie is on the football team. Joining a team can be a great way to meet new people, because you have a built-in subject to talk about! Plus, you can always invite a teammate to hang out after practice, or suggest getting together on the weekends to practice your sport. Bonus: you'll get plenty of exercise!

✳ **Volunteer.** Betty loves to volunteer—whether it's to help plant a community garden, walk the dogs at the local shelter, or teach kids how to read. It can be a great way to meet

people who live close to you—besides, people who volunteer tend to be really nice. Bonus: when you're helping people or animals, you can feel good about what you're doing!

✳ **Start a book club.** If you love to read, starting a book club can be a great way to discover great new books. Talk to your librarian about your book club—let her know that you'll want to meet at the library. Then ask her to help you put up a flyer calling for members who are close to your age. Once a month, you'll meet to discuss the book you've all read, and then come up with a book to read for the next month. You'll meet a lot of different people—and you'll always have something to talk about. Bonus: if you mention your club to your teacher you may just get extra credit!

Betty's Tips for Making Friends if You're New

🌸 **Smile!** Sure, when you're new, you may not feel like smiling. But a friendly, open expression signals that you're ready to make friends. Nobody wants to try to talk to a grouch!

🌸 **Ask for help.** If you want to meet people, find out what they're good at, and ask for their help. This can be as simple as asking them to show you around your new school.

🌸 **Give compliments.** If you like someone's shirt, hat, bag, or whatever—go ahead and say so! Everyone loves a little praise. And sometimes a compliment can lead to lots of fun!

🌸 **Take a risk!** Trying something new can be a great way to make friends. If you've always wanted to try karate, learn to ice-skate, or act in a play, now is the time to go for it!

🌸 **Be yourself.** Don't pretend to be interested in something you're not in order to meet people. It takes time, but eventually you'll meet a bunch of people who like you for you.

Cool Conversation-Starters When There's a New Kid in School

So the new girl looks interesting—and she's reading the very same book you are. You'd think you had a lot in common, but you're not sure what to say. Try one of these surefire ways to get to know her. She'll probably be glad you did!

✧ **Ask questions.** Find out where she's from, whether she has sisters and brothers, whether she has any pets, and what her favorite movies are. It's an easy way to get to know someone!

✧ **Tell her what you like to do on the weekend.** Then ask her what she likes to do. You might find that you could be doing some of those things together!

✧ **Clue her in!** Remember that new kids don't know which teachers are toughest, which foods to avoid in the cafeteria, or which water fountains are out of order. She'll be grateful for any tips you can offer.

☼ **Ask if she wants to get together to study.** Hey, if she's in your class, then she's got the same homework that you do—and you're both going to have to do it sometime. And you know what they say—two heads are better than one!

☼ **Invite her to sit with you at lunch.** Being the new kid can be hard . . . especially at lunch or recess, when everyone is with their groups of friends. And if you can't think of anything to talk about—there's always food! Find out her favorites (and least favorites), and share your own!

Ronnie's Tips for When You're Feeling Shy

Whether it's on a team, at school, or in the neighborhood, everyone is new at some point. What do you do if you're feeling shy? It isn't easy to make new friends. Let me give you a few of my no-fail pointers.

1. Remember that you're the world's only fabulous you! Make a list of everything you're good at and/or enjoy doing. Dance? Drawing? Baseball? Cooking? Okay! Now you have a whole list of ways to meet people!

2. Don't hide! You might think that it's easier to hole up in your room than to make new friends. The only problem is—it can get lonely! Sometimes, you may have to force yourself to get out there and talk to people. But once you do it, you'll find that it's a lot easier than you thought.

3. Remember that everyone feels shy sometimes. But other people want to make new friends, too! (Hey—everybody likes to be liked!) So all you're doing is making the first move. They (and you) will be glad you did.

4. Lead with your strength. If you're a super soccer player or an excellent singer, try to join groups where you can really shine. If you're confident in what you're doing, other people will see that and admire it.

5. Set a goal. For example, maybe you can try talking to one new person a day. By the end of the school week, you'll know five new people! You don't have to have a long conversation. Even something like, "Did you write down the homework assignment?" can be enough to break the ice.

What NOT to Say if You're the New Kid

★ What do you people do for fun around here?

★ My old school was way better, because _____. (Even if it's true!)

★ What's so great about this town?

★ You smell funky.

★ I hate it here.

★ Everyone at this school dresses weird.

★ Nobody liked me at my old school, either.

Boy Friend
vs. Boyfriend

Having a guy friend is different from having a girl friend. Note the basic physical differences.

Topics That Generally Make Guys Roll Their Eyes

Of course, not all guys are the same. But here are a few things you probably want to avoid talking about with most of your guy friends. . . .

1. Makeup
2. Cute guys you're crushin' on
3. Fashion
4. Celebrity gossip
5. Who has a crush on whom in your class
6. Your ideal wedding
7. Hairstyles
8. Nail-polish shades
9. Underwear
10. Movies that make you cry

Topics That Are Okay for Most Guys

1. Food
2. Cars
3. Food and cars
4. Video games
5. Music
6. Sports
7. Extreme sports
8. Scary movies
9. Extremely scary movies
10. Watching an extremely scary movie with a cool sound track while playing an extreme sports video game and eating a hamburger

Recommended Lines to Use When People Tease You About Your "Boyfriend"

Even though Ronnie is kidding, it *can* be kind of a pain to have a guy friend—especially if your other friends like to tease you about being a couple when you're not. But it can also be really great. Any new friend will have his or her own take on things . . . and guys often have very different perspectives. A guy friend can give you a new way to see yourself and the people around you. So if your other friends start hassling you for hanging with him, here are some things you can tell them.

- He's not my boyfriend, he's my friend-boy.
- I know we're both pretty irresistible, but—really—we're just pals.
- Don't say that! I want Josh Hartnett to know I'm available!
- We like each other a lot . . . but not in that way.
- We're *friends* . . . you know, as in, people who don't give each other a hard time?

Problems with Your Guy Friend

Okay, so that was the plus side. But having a guy friend isn't always ideal. Sometimes, they can do things that drive you crazy. Here are a few problems that I've had to deal with, and ways that I have handled them.

♡ **He takes "my house is your house" a little too far.** Your guy friend loves to hang out at your house . . . where he gobbles down everything—including the coconut cookies your dad made for dessert! He puts his feet on the coffee table and watches sports for hours, then doesn't clean up the popcorn that lands all over the floor when he cheers that final touchdown. What to do?

Remedy: Sometimes, a guy will feel so comfortable hanging at your house that he forgets that he's a guest. Gentle reminders work best. The next time he makes a mess, say, "Why don't you help me clean up before you take off?" And if certain foods are off-limits, let him know ahead of time. You may even want to suggest that he bring some of his favorite snacks along with him when he comes. Clear off a shelf in the pantry, and label it for him, so that he can keep it stocked himself.

But the good part is . . .

If your guy friend feels comfortable at your house, it's probably because he really digs hanging with you. Besides, sometimes it's fun to be casual. You can dress like a slob and eat like a pig, and you know your guy won't care. In fact, he'll probably love it!

♡ **He complains that you're too "girlie."** It seems as though everything you say—from your opinion on J.Lo to your fashion critiques of the girl in the back row to your list of favorite movies—makes him complain that you're being girlie. Well, you're a girl, right? What are you supposed to do about it?

Remedy: It's all about compromise. Point out all of the stuff that he does that's too "guy-ish"—all of the times you have to listen to his descriptions of action movies, the times you sit watching him play video games, and the times he demands that you join him to watch professional wrestling. Agree to trade off sometimes. You get fifteen minutes of girlie stuff for every fifteen of his guy-ish stuff. You want to watch a chick flick? Fine. You'll pay for it—with an hour and a half of televised BMX racing.

But the good part is . . .

At least you know he'll never criticize your outfits or go after your crush!

♡ **He takes over.** The minute you two sit down, he grabs the remote and starts flipping—and completely ignores you when you say, "Stop—I want to watch this." He always wants to decide what you'll do together. You suggest ice-skating—he wants to go sledding. You suggest Frisbee—he wants to play basketball. He suffers from in-charge-itis, and it's driving you nuts!

Remedy: He probably doesn't realize that he's being bossy. The next time he starts to take over, call him on it. Point out that he picked the TV show, or movie, or activity, or *whatever,* the last time, and now it's your turn. Usually, guys want things to be fair. If you give it to him straight, he'll respect you for it.

But the good part is . . .

Guys like this are usually down for having fun. They're bossy because they have a million interests in their lives—and that keeps *your* life interesting!

♡ He punches you on the shoulder—hard!

He thinks that he's just being playful, but those friendly little pats leave you black and blue. You don't mind horsing around sometimes . . . you just don't want to feel like a punching bag!

Remedy: Guys wrestle with each other all the time. Your guy probably just doesn't realize his own strength. Let him know that he's actually hurting you when he roughhouses. If he doesn't get the message, you may have to rethink your friendship. It just isn't worth the pain!

But the good part is . . .

If he's that strong, you can get him to haul heavy stuff around for you! This could come in handy the next time you're lugging home a stack of books for that history project.

What If Your Feelings Turn Romantic?

You and your guy friend have been pals for years. But lately, your girlfriends are complaining that you talk about him way too much. You've noticed that you've been spendin a lot of time wondering if he thinks you're funny and pretty. And you've been feeling jealous when he mentions other girls. Oh, no! Could you be feeling *that way* about hi Well—why not? Crushing on a guy friend make perfect sense. After all, you already like him— otherwise he wouldn't be your friend, right? Bu can be a complicated situation. Here's the rund

Pros

* You already like him.
* You know he's sweet.
* You get along great.
* You feel comfortable around him.

Cons

* You could lose the friendship!
* You could embarrass yourself.

You're probably asking yourself if it's worth it to let him know how you feel. Well—how do you think he feels about *you*? If you think the crush is mutual, then you might want to consider telling him about your feelings.

Things can turn awkward when one person feels romantic and the other doesn't. If you think your crush is heading only one way down that two-way street, you can try getting him to see you in a different light—if you usually chill out in a group, try spending more one-on-one time together. If you often do one-on-one things, see if you can make things seem more datelike by heading out to the movies or dinner. Then give it time, and see where it goes. Sometimes, it just takes guys a while to realize that their feelings are changing, too.

Friend-Filled Activities

It's Your Friend's Special Day!

So it's your good friend's birthday, but you aren't sure what to get her. You've come to the right place! I always pick out the absolute best presents. Just choose anything from the list below, and I'm sure your friend will be the happiest girl in town!

Veronica's List of Fabulous Presents

- A day at the most exclusive spa in town
- A diamond necklace
- A trip to Paris, Rome, or the Caribbean
- A pedigreed poodle
- A designer gown
- A carriage ride around Central Park after a Broadway show (It's even more special if you don't live in New York!)

Not all of us have Mr. Lodge backing us up in buying our friends' gifts. If you're like me, and your budget is a little on the small side, here are some ideas for gifts that won't break the bank.

Happy-Thoughts Jar

Check your family's recycling bin for a good-sized jar, with or without a lid. Clean the jar well, with warm, soapy water. If the jar has a label, soak it in hot water for fifteen minutes—the label should peel off easily. Once the jar is clean, use stickers and paint pens to decorate it, and write the words *Happy-Thoughts Jar* on the outside. Then cruise the Internet, the library, and your bookshelf for poems, sayings, famous quotations, and words of wisdom about friendship, love, and happy things. Write the quotes down on small slips of paper, and place the happy thoughts inside the jar for your friend to pull out whenever she needs a lift. It's a gift that keeps surprising your friend and shows how much you care!

Sweet-Dreams Pillowcase

All you need in order to make this gift is a plain pillowcase in a light or bright color (preferably your friend's favorite) and a few fabric-markers. Decorate the pillowcase with all of your best friend's hopes, dreams, and favorite things—for example, the name of her celebrity crushes, the name of her dream college, the city where she wants to live, and a list of her favorite foods, movies, books, and bands. When her head hits the pillow at night, she'll think of you and all your good thoughts. It's a surefire way to keep nightmares at bay!

Personalized Cupcakes

Get an adult to help you bake up a batch of your friend's favorite-flavor cupcakes. Then, while they cool, sit down and make a list of all of your friend's best qualities. Is she funny? Smart? Thoughtful? Athletic? Once you have your list, frost the cupcakes. Then get a tube of icing in a different color and write one kind word on each cupcake. It's a sweet gift for a sweet friend—one that each of your friends will enjoy!

Decorated Locker

Get out streamers, glitter, signs, and balloons, and go crazy glamming up your friend's locker before school starts. Slide a card through the vents, so that it will be there when your friend opens her locker. Then wait nearby to see the huge smile on her face!

Fun Through the Year

Get a plain wall calendar, and go through the months, marking down special dates—and a few random ones—where you might plan to do things together with your friend. During the summer, you can schedule a swimming date for you and your friend. During the winter, maybe you could go ice-skating. Mark each special date with colorful pens and stickers, so that your friend knows she can look forward to a year full of fun with you!

Even if it isn't anyone's birthday, there are all sorts of reasons to have fun and get together with friends. Here are a few excuses to hang out and have a good time:

January: *New Year, Old Friends.* Plan a casual get-together with your best bud and a few others on New Year's Day. Remember all of the fun things you did together the year before, and make plans for the upcoming year.

February: *Valentine's Day.* Hey, Valentine's Day doesn't have to be all about romance. You and your friends can hang out, exchange cards, and eat candy together! Go around the

60

room and say your favorite things about each person for an instant friend-love pick-me-up!

March: *St. Patrick's Day Treasure Hunt.* Get all of your best buds together for a treasure hunt. (Be sure to ask for parental permission first, of course!) The treasure might be a big bowl of candy, the video you're going to watch that night, or any other prize you can think of. A few days before the party, take a tour of your house or neighborhood and make a list of the things you see. Then make a list of those things for your friends to find. Once your guests arrive, divide them into two teams, and give each team a list of things to find in the house or in the neighborhood—like a red leaf, a round-faced clock, or a red gnome. The first team to find everything on the list wins!

April/May: *Spring Fling.* Spend an afternoon with your friend planting flowers to celebrate spring. If you don't have your own garden, there are lots of community planting projects that could use volunteers. Ask at your school or community center if there are any projects that need kids to help out.

June: *No More Pencils!* On the last day of school, go out with your friends for a School's-Out snack. Burgers or ice cream cones are ideal to get you in the spirit of summer!

July/August: *Summer Fun!* Plan an afternoon at the beach or pool with your best buds. Or pack a cooler with sodas and sandwiches, and have a picnic at the park— or even in the backyard! (That way, you don't have to go very far for refills on lemonade!)

September: *Back-to-School Blast.* Before school starts, ask all of your buds to pick out cool pens, pencils, notebooks, and erasers.

Then host a swap! People can barter one of their erasers for one of your purple pens. You'll all show up at school with the funkiest accessories in the halls.

October: *Halloween—Dress as Each Other!* If you're always desperate to come up with a good costume, think about dressing as each other for the holiday. Swap your favorite clothes, and giggle as people try to guess who you are!

November: *Welcome Fall!* Invite a friend to go apple-picking, then ask your parent or guardian to help the two of you bake a pie or make applesauce. It's a great way to gear up for Thanksgiving.

December: *Secret Santa!* Leave little gifts or treats for your friends without letting them know who's doing it. (You could even leave a few for yourself, so they don't get suspicious.) Then have fun as they all try to guess who their Secret Santas could be!

Friends and Boyfriend Blues

Crush Triangle

> Veronica and I are sort of experts on this subject! It can be fun when you and your best friend are eyeing the same guy—you can discuss all of the cute things he says and does, and keep an eye out for other girls who might be crushing on him, too. What should you do when you're faced with a crush triangle? Here are a few tips:

If you're the one he likes:

1. *Be sensitive.* Your friend is probably heartsick right now . . . and to make matters worse, she's also probably worried that you're going to start spending all of your time with your new boyfriend instead of her! Try to call your friend often and spend plenty of time with her, so she knows that you aren't going to disappear.

2. *Don't accuse your friend of not being happy for you.* No matter how much she loves you, your friend is dealing with a lot of tough emotions right now. Try to understand how *she's* feeling . . . once she is okay with things, you can try to work out a way to face the sticky situation. In time, you can both be happy.

3. *Don't spend all of your time talking about your new guy!* Sure, you and your friend are used to gossiping about his every move. But if he's started liking you back, your hourly updates may start to seem like insensitive bragging. Find something else to talk about— like shopping, sports, or school.

4. *Give her time.* It takes a while to mend a broken heart. Don't expect your friend to snap out of it and find a new crush right away. It *will* happen eventually . . . and when it does, then you can look forward to those double dates!

If your friend is the one he likes:

1. *Try to understand.* Your friend is probably very excited about her new guy. She may want to talk about him now and then. Try not to feel upset if she does. She isn't trying to hurt your feelings—she's just excited and wants to tell you about what's going on in her life.

2. *Don't take it personally.* Just because he's interested in your friend, it doesn't mean that there's something wrong with you. Liking someone is all about making the right connection.

You may be just as pretty, smart, and funny as your friend—but if his feelings just aren't there for you, your crush won't be mutual.

3. *Don't blame your friend.* Try to put yourself in her shoes: if your crush liked *you*, you wouldn't tell him to get lost just because your friend liked him, too, would you? Remember that she didn't steal him from you—you both liked him, and now he's noticed one of you. That's the way these things happen sometimes.

4. *Don't forget that there are other boys out there.* I know, I know—but *this* is the one you wanted! Once you get over feeling that way, though, you'll start to see why you and your crush boy wouldn't have worked together anyway. Then you can keep an eye out for one of those other cuties. If your girlfriend is going out with your crush, maybe she can find a cute friend for *you.* . . .

Betty on Making Up with Your Best Bud

Arguing is part of what friends do. But making up can be hard to do after a major blowout. If you end up on the wrong side of a friendsplosion, here are some creative ways to tell your best bud that you're sorry.

⭐ **Make it musical.** Make up a song and leave it on her answering machine. The sillier the better! When she stops laughing, she'll have to forgive you.

⭐ **Get things cookin'.** Bake a batch of her favorite brownies or cookies. Use a small tube of colored frosting to decorate the treats with the words "I'm sorry," then head over to her house. Sometimes, all it takes is something sweet to wash the bitterness away.

⭐ **You've got mail.** Get out the old construction paper, doilies, and scissors to make your best bud a valentine . . . even if it's the middle of July. Be sure to say how much the friendship means to you, then slip the card into her mailbox.

Furry
(or Feathered or
Fishy) Friends

A pet can make a great friend! Personally, I love having a dog. Sometimes it seems as if he's part of the family. I'm sure Betty would tell you that it's a great way to get exercise and spend time outdoors. But of course, the reason I love having a dog is that it's a great way to meet guys! When they stop to pet my poodle, I start to flirt. A pet is a no-fail guy magnet.

Here are a few other reasons why a dog makes a great friend:

1. Will fetch for fun
2. Loves to give kisses
3. Never steals your boyfriend
4. Knows when to obey
5. Always makes a good-looking escort
6. Never hogs the phone
7. Always has time to listen to your problems
8. Won't ditch you to go on a date
9. Always takes your call
10. Never tells you when you're having a bad-hair day

My cats and I are very close. There's nobody I'd rather cuddle up with on a cold night. Besides, they never complain when my room is a mess! Some people think that cats aren't friendly, but I don't think that's true. My kitties love to be petted, and will sit on my lap, purring, for hours. Sometimes my human friends forget to tell me that they appreciate me—but my cats always let me know!

Here are a few other reasons why a cat makes a great friend:

1. Makes a great foot warmer
2. Never too busy to hang out
3. Won't talk back
4. Never has a party without asking you first
5. Knows how to keep a secret
6. Never borrows your stuff without asking
7. Won't talk during a movie (or steal your popcorn, either!)
8. Purrs at your jokes
9. Never gripes about your cooking
10. Never complains when you want to spend time with your other friends

When you have a pet, you want to spend special time with it every day. They love to have treats now and then. Here are a few ideas to show your special pal how much you care:

Give your dog a special, yummy, high-protein treat. Take one of your doggy's favorite biscuits and slather it with peanut butter—then watch as your pet devours the treat! (Don't give your dog too many treats, though. One biscuit once in a while is plenty to keep him happy.)

Make a fun and easy kitty toy. Find a stick about three feet long. Cut a six-foot length of yarn, and tie it securely to the stick. Use the stick to dangle the yarn in front of your cat—make it dance and flitter all over the room! This is excellent exercise for your cat—and lots of fun for both of you!

Give your bird a box of raisins. Fruit is a tasty treat for birds. Buy some super-small packages of raisins, and put one box in your bird's cage. Let your bird open the box and discover the treats inside!

Make a play box for your guinea pig. Fill a large shoe box with paper-towel and toilet-paper tubes. Let your guinea pig tear through them—it's like a rec room for your furry friend!

What If Your Family Won't Let You Have a Pet?

> If you want a special friend but your family says no, here are a few ideas.

Consider an "easy" pet. Sometimes parents are concerned that a pet will be too much work. Other times, a family member has allergies that make a furry pet out of the question. If this is the case in your family, consider getting a freshwater fish or a turtle. These pets take much less work than a dog, and won't make you sneeze.

Volunteer at an animal hospital or a shelter. Your local shelter would probably be thrilled to have your help! Get your parents' permission to volunteer. Then ask around or go online to find out where the best shelters are in the neighborhood. You don't want to work for a shelter where the animals aren't treated well! Call the shelter, asking if they need volunteers. Soon, you'll have more cats and dogs than you know what to do with! (And you'll be working to find a good home for animals.)

Adopt your friend's pet for a day. Take your friend's dog to the park or dog run. Make sure to take along Fido's favorite toys and treats, of course! This can be a great way to get to know different breeds of dog and see which one is your favorite.

Pet-sit. If you have a friend with a small pet (a guinea pig, bird, or gerbil, for example), offer to take care of the pet the next time your friend is out of town. (Be sure to ask your parents first if it's okay, of course.) It's a great way to see what it's like to take care of a pet—without commitment.

Set up an outdoor bird-feeder. This is a great way to watch colorful birds from a distance. Check online to see what birds live in your area, and what they like to eat. Then ask your parents for help setting up the feeder outside your window.

Pet Dos and Don'ts

[✔] **Don't** just bring home a pet. You're hoping that once your parents see that dog or cat, they'll love it just as much as you do. But your whole family is going to have to live with the pet—so the decision will involve more than just you. Besides, if your parents say no to your having a pet, they probably have a good reason.

[✔] **Don't** forget that a pet is like part of the family. Taking care of an animal is a big commitment, and you have to make sure that everyone is committed to making your pet happy and comfortable in your home.

[✔] **Don't** ignore allergies. Some people can develop serious breathing problems if they are around animals. This can be hard to accept when you really, really want a dog—but ignoring allergies can be dangerous.

[✔] **Don't** forget that a pet needs a lot of your time and attention. Yes, cats and dogs are cute and furry. But they require care. If you spend most of your day away from home, involved with various activities, you may not have enough time for a pet.

[✔] Do make sure you know what you're getting into. Pets are time-consuming. That's why the whole family has to get involved in helping out. With your family, discuss the jobs involved in taking care of your new pet—and agree on who will take on which duties. That way, no one will get stuck with more work than anybody else.

[✔] Do pick the right pet! You may fall in love with that adorable golden retriever puppy . . . but it's going to grow up to be a very large dog! If you live in an apartment, or a house without a yard, you might want to consider a smaller breed of dog, or a cat. Also remember that some dogs bark more than others—and that that can annoy neighbors.

[✔] Do learn about the pet before bringing it home. That way, you can have the proper bed, toys, and treats on hand when your pet comes home with you. You'll also know what to feed it, what might make it sick, and what to do in case of an emergency.

Friends
Forever

Differences— *Dos and Don'ts*

I love Ronnie. But our friendship isn't always easy. She can be a little competitive. Like when she tries to hog Archie all to herself. (Everyone knows he's perfect for me!) There are going to be times when your friend drives you crazy. Here are a few common problems and ways to deal with them.

You can be different from your best friend and still be best friends!

Problem: we have different interests.

This is something that comes up between Ronnie and me all of the time. I like to play basketball—she hates to sweat. I like to cook—she doesn't know what a ladle is. I like to fix cars—she doesn't even like to open the car door for herself. What can you do when it seems as if you and your best friend never want to do the same thing at the same time?

Betty sez: Don't give up on someone just because you've got different interests. Maybe you need to get out of your rut. Talk to your friend and tell her how you are feeling. Then you can try to find some all-new things to do together that will make you both happy. If that doesn't work, try trading off—you go in-line skating one day, she goes to the movies another. Or find things that you both have in common. For me and Ronnie, there's always shopping, the beach, and boy-watching! (Or all three at once!)

Remember:

DO work to keep the friendship alive.

DON'T try to give your friend a personality makeover, or agree to do things that you aren't interested in. There has to be some common ground for the both of you!

Problem: she's a mooch!

Oh, I have this problem all the time. After all, Daddykins has lots of money—and he never minds (much) when I use my credit cards to treat my friends to some fun. But there was a time when Jughead came over and ate up all of the refreshments before Daddy's big gala dinner. That was a bad night—for Jughead! If you have a friend who borrows like there's no tomorrow, then you know what I'm talking about. Sure, you want your friend to feel like your things are her things . . . just maybe not so much!

Veronica sez: Ask yourself this: how much does this moochy behavior really bother you— and how one-sided is it? Some people don't mind sharing—and maybe you have a few of *her* magazines on your shelf and some of her sweaters in your closet, too. If the sharing seems like a two-way street, it may not be a problem. But if it's not, you'll have to confront your friend. Tell her that you want your things back eventually—and that her borrowing habits make you feel as though she's using you. A real friend will understand . . . and apologize. When it came to Jughead, though, I just had to accept that if we were going to be friends, I'd just have to stock some extra snacks. So I did—and Daddy never had another problem with any of his dinner parties!

Remember:

DO understand that she may simply admire your taste.

DON'T let her treat you like a doormat. Stand up for yourself!

Problem: she's stealing your thunder!

When Cheryl Blossom showed up at our school, I thought that Ronnie was going to pitch a fit. After all, Ronnie had always been the most stylish girl in school . . . until Cheryl came along. Do you have a friend who likes to do everything you do . . . better? If you're brainy, she's brainier. If you can sing, she can sing louder. Sure, good friends should have things in common . . . but you want to be the best at *something*!

Betty sez: Try to think about the positive side—at least the two of you have tons in common! And—once you get over feeling jealous, which is perfectly natural, by the way—you can probably learn a thing or two from your friend. Take Ronnie, for example. She and Cheryl both had so much style that they should have started their own fashion line! If the two of them ever joined forces, they'd be unstoppable!

Remember:

DO try to be the best that you can be . . . and accept that you'll always be better at some things than other people are—and that others will be better at some things than you.

DON'T compete with her nonstop. You'll drive each other crazy!

Problem: she steals your guy.

Once I was sitting on the couch with Archie when Betty came in to tell me that I had a phone call. So I got up to answer the phone, but there was nobody on the line. And by the time I got back to the couch, Betty had taken my place, next to Archie! Do you have a friend who's always after your guy?

Veronica sez: Even though Betty and I both like Archie, we manage to be friends, but it isn't easy. You have to start by being honest with your friend. Tell her that it hurts your feelings that she seems to want to compete with you over guys. Listen to what she says. She may not even realize what she's doing!

Remember:

DO admire her taste in guys.

DON'T try to get even by stealing her guy—you'll end up in a huge mess!

Problem: your friend is moving away.

I remember the time I thought that Veronica was going away to boarding school. At first, I was excited because I thought I'd have Archie all to myself. But the more I thought about it, the more I realized just how much I was going to miss my best friend.

Betty sez: I've never been more relieved than I was the moment I heard that Ronnie wasn't moving away, after all. But I'd already thought of all of the great ways that we could keep in touch—like writing each other weekly e-mails and sending funny cards.

Remember:

DO make a plan with your friend for ways you can keep in touch.

DON'T blame your friend if she's really busy for a few weeks after her move and doesn't have time to write. It can take time to settle into a new home.

Talk, Talk, Talk!

> My parents are always asking me why I need to chat on the phone with my friends all night when I've just spent all day with them at school. We're talking about what we did that day, of course! It's important to keep in touch on a daily, if not hourly, basis, so Ronnie and I have worked up a few ideas for those of you who understand the need to reach out to your friends.

Create a Friend Blog

If you like to write, a friend blog can be a great way to keep in touch. Simply spend a few minutes every day writing up something funny that happened to you or your friends, and send it out via e-mail to your closest buds. Ask them to do the same thing. At the end of the year, you'll have a record of everything that has happened to all of you. You can print it out and make copies for your closest friends, as keepsakes. It's way better than writing "Have a great summer!" in their yearbooks.

Create a Memory Box

You'll need a shoe box, white paste, and some magazines or photos for this project. Go through the magazines and tear out any images that remind you of your friend. If she's into nature, sports, movies, music, or fashion, this should be easy! (You can also use photos of you and your friends, if you have enough.) Cut out the pictures and paste them to the outsides and insides of the box. Wait for the paste to dry, then start collecting objects that bring back memories of the year—maybe a seashell from a day the two of you went to the beach, a dried friendship flower, or a valentine. At the end of the year (or on your friend's birthday), present her with the memory box. She'll never forget you!

Make a Photo Album

This is an especially good project if you've been friends for a long time. Go through your piles of pictures and choose photos of you and your friend. Place them in an album, and write down what you were doing in each picture. Then get together with your friend to write funny captions on small slips of paper, and place them next to the pictures. You can also place movie stubs, concert tickets, paper menus from restaurants you've been to together, and other things in the album along with the photos—just make sure that you explain what they are. You and your friend can add to the album whenever you have a new memory to share!

How You Know She's Your Best Friend

Both Ronnie and I have a ton of friends—but when it comes to being best friends, we don't need anyone but each other. Sometimes I think Ronnie knows me even better than I know myself! So—how do we do it, year after year? What does it take to be a best friend? I'll bet you already know the answer. But just in case, here's one final list. . . .

♥ She's the first person you call when you have a problem.

♥ She can finish your sentences.

♥ You know you can count on her to keep a secret.

♥ She would never let you walk around with your hair sticking up, with something in your teeth, or with your fly unzipped (she'd tell you).

♥ When something special happens to her, she wants you to be the first person to know.

♥ You don't even have to make plans—your hang time is set in stone.

♥ She'll tell you the truth when your outfit is kind of . . . off. (But she won't be rude about it!)

♥ You spend so much time on the phone together your parents joke that the receiver may get permanently stuck to your ear.

♥ You know the names of all of her crushes, past and present.

♥ You'd stick up for her no matter what—and vice versa.

♥ You forgive her . . . even when she tries to steal your Archie!